SHED

Amber's first day in New Havelock.
Six months after her father fell in a hole.

By Richard Fairgray
& Lucy Campagnolo

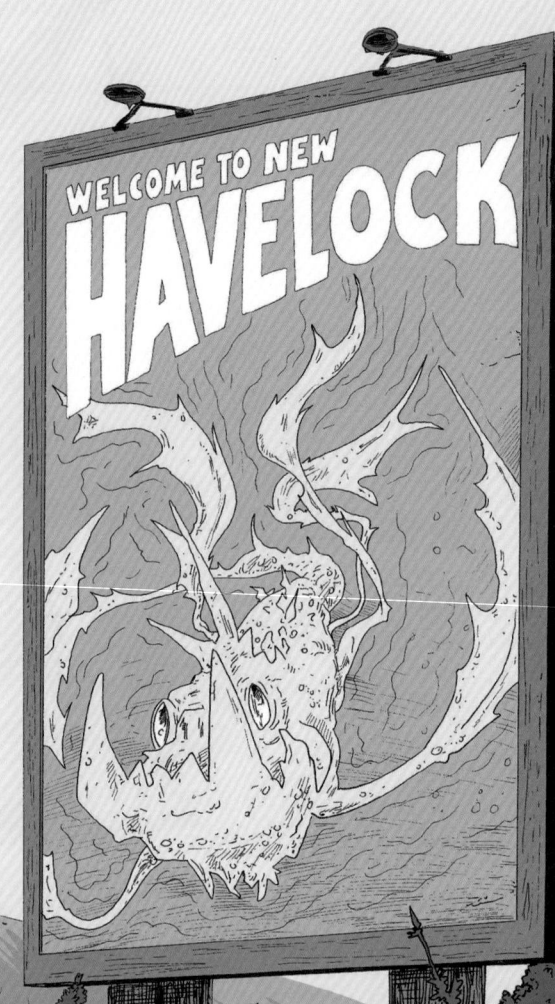

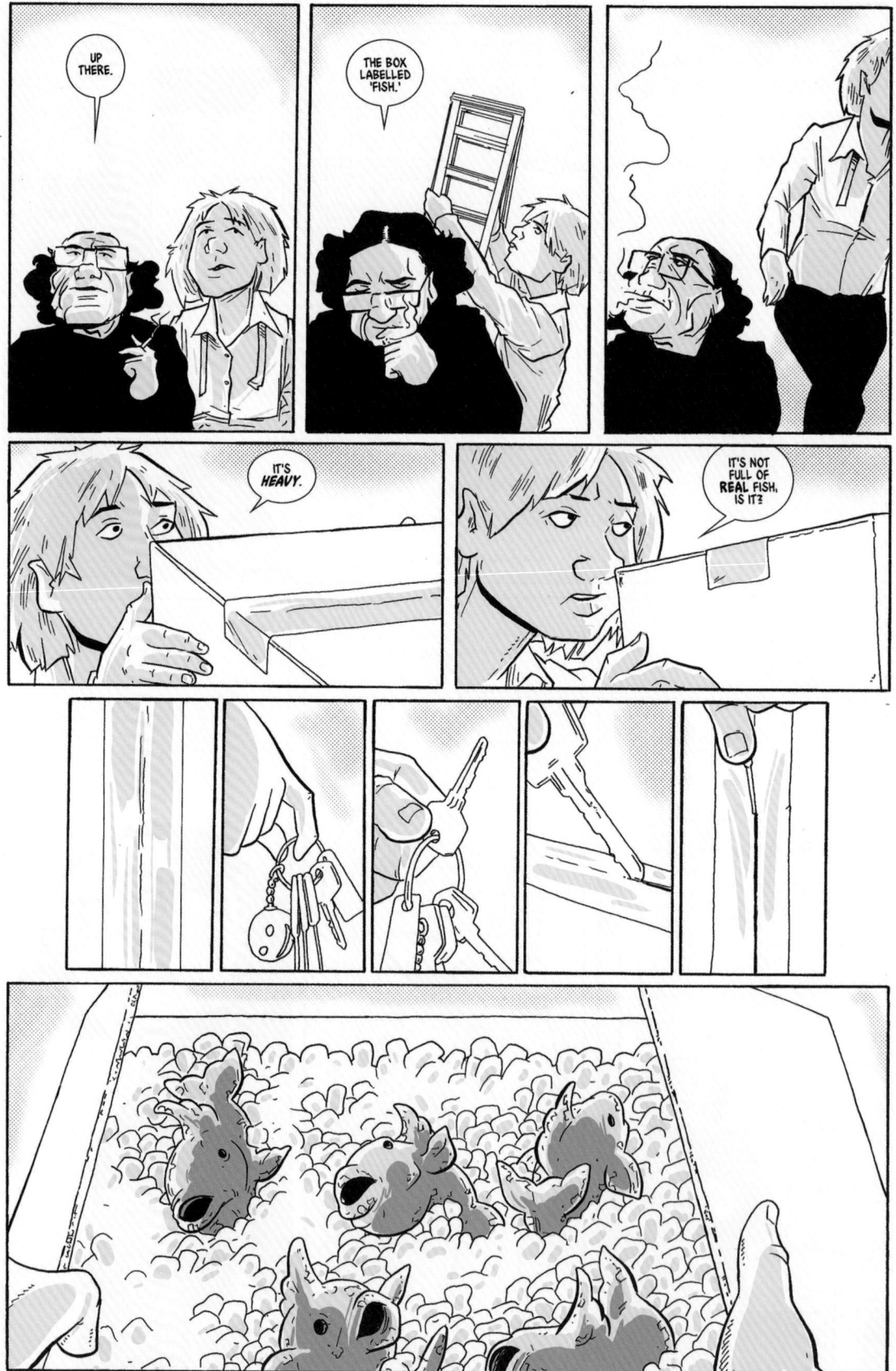

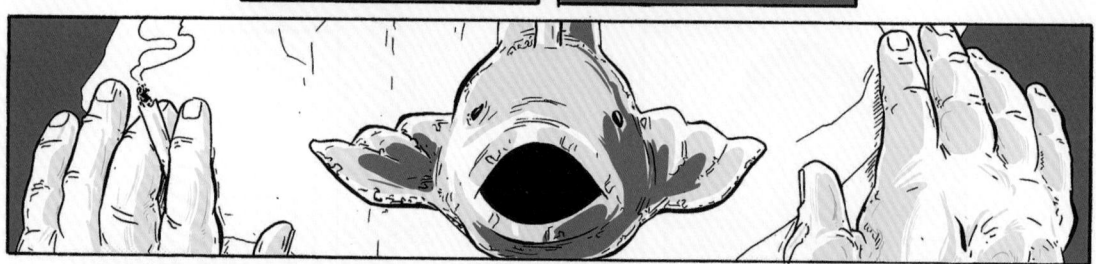

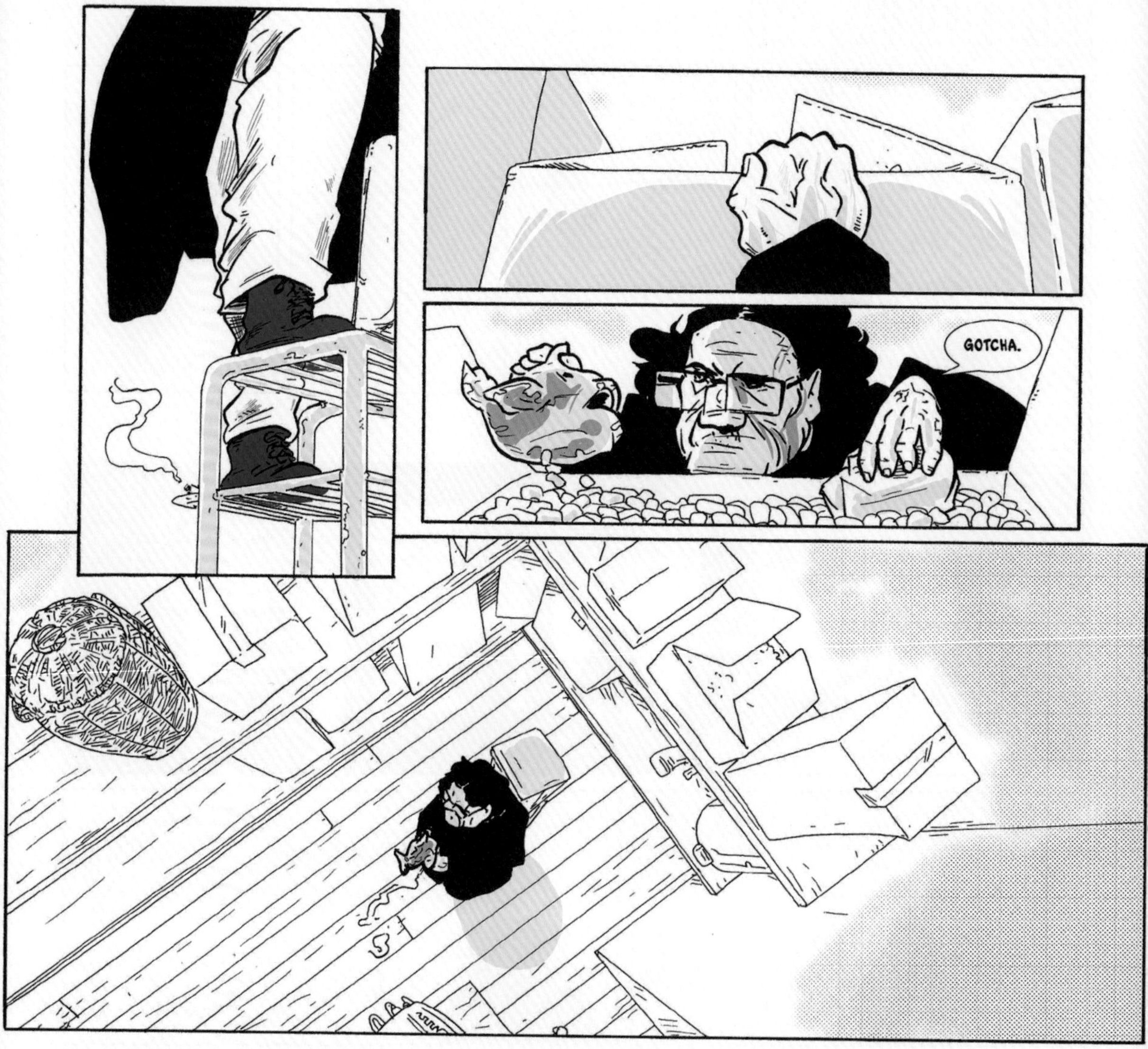

BUH-LUH-LULULUL

BUH-LUH-LULULUL

WHO CALLS A FUCKING LANDLINE?

TO BE CONTINUED.

SHED

3

The Sunday that followed the Saturday when Amber asked Fran if they could still be in cahoots.

By Richard Fairgray
& Lucy Campagnolo

SHED

The night that Mildred and Fran burnt down the pier..

Ten years before Amber's father fell in a hole.

By Richard Fairgray
& Lucy Campagnolo

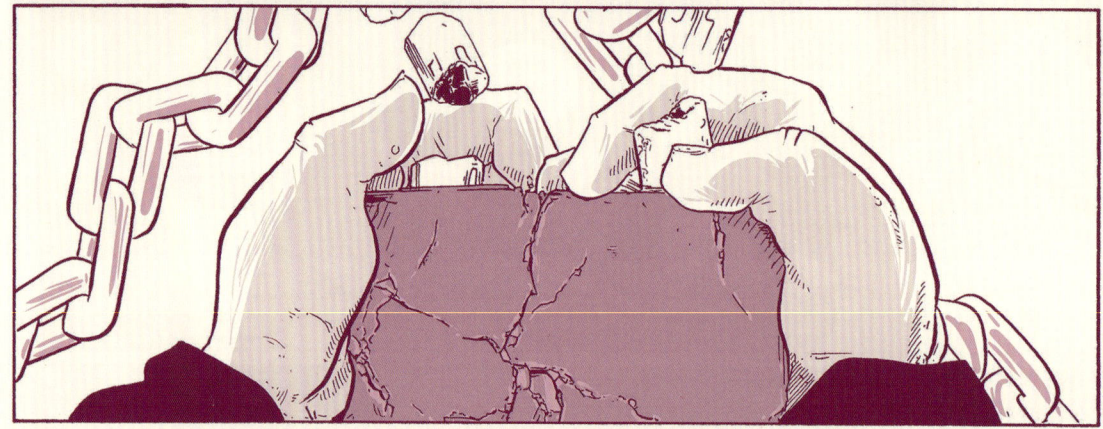

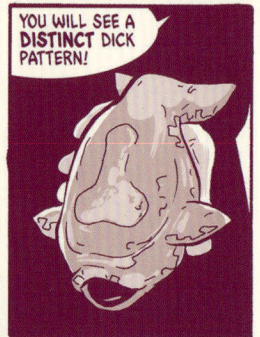
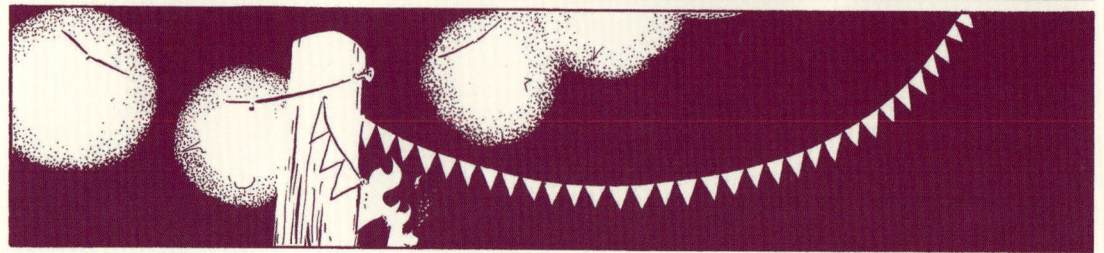

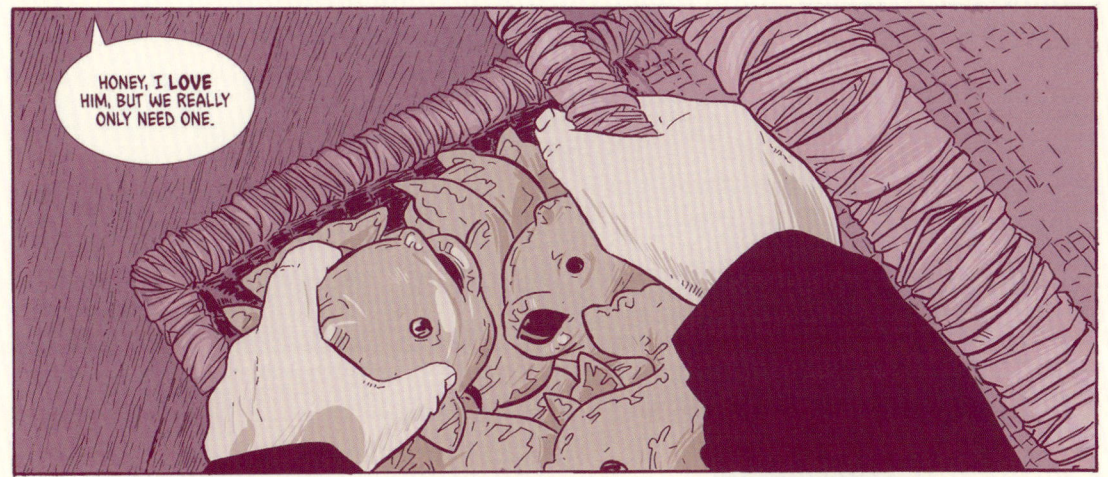

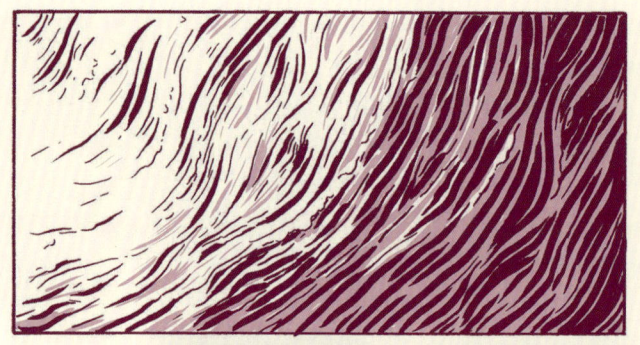

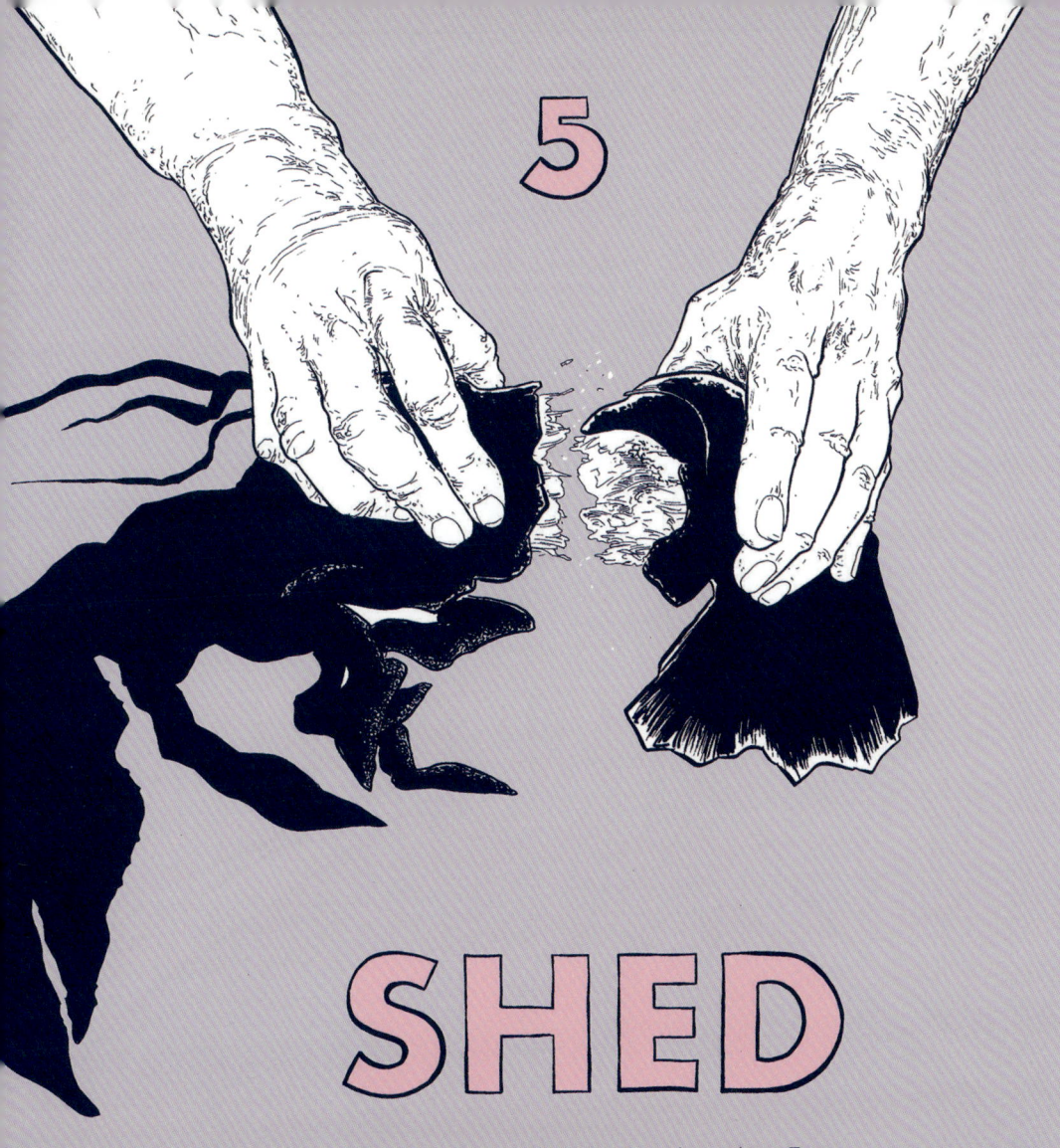

5

SHED

The Thursday after the Sunday when Fran and Amber failed to retrieve the fish.

The day of the will reading.

By Richard Fairgray
& Lucy Campagnolo

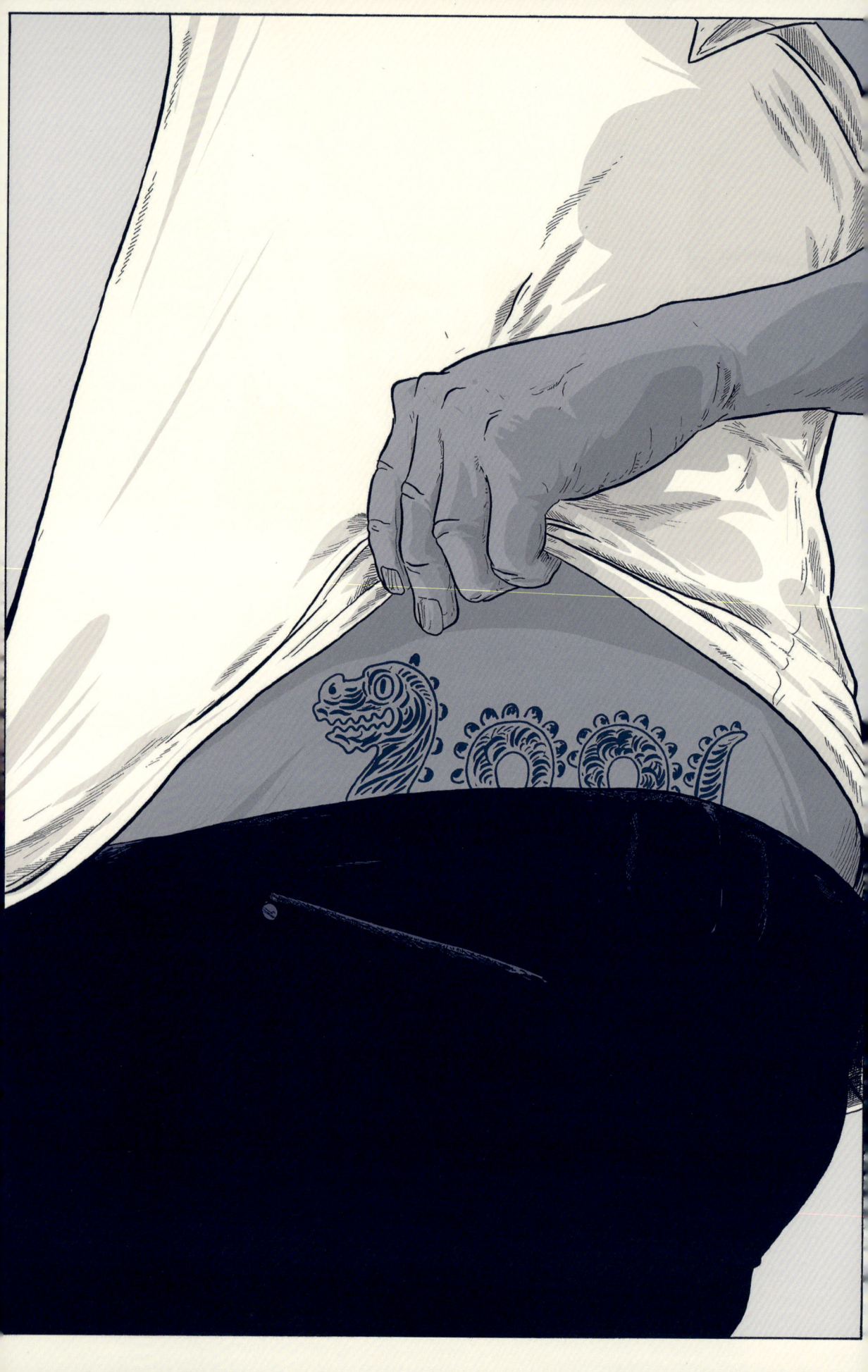

"None of you even know!" the girl yelled, more shocked than angry. "Have any of you ever actually seen it?!"

And, of course, none of them ever had.

So, the girl set out to see the sea monster for herself.

She ran to the shore to where the boats lay idle, but they'd all been there for too long, and the sand had buried them.

Anyone else might have given up, but the girl picked up a piece of driftwood and began building a path out into the sea.

She gathered every stick, branch and board she could find and slowly but surely the path began to take shape.

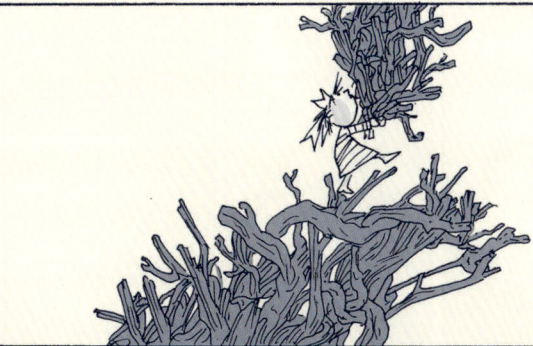

"Hello," said the girl.

And just like that, the monster that had stopped people from leaving became the thing that everybody wanted to see.

The little town with the pathway into the ocean where the girl had met a sea monster.

All thanks to one person's curiosity, the town was alive again.

TO BE CONTINUED.

6

SHED

One year since Amber's father fell down a hole.

Six months since Fran disappeared.

Six months since Amber got that bad advice.

By Richard Fairgray & Lucy Campagnolo

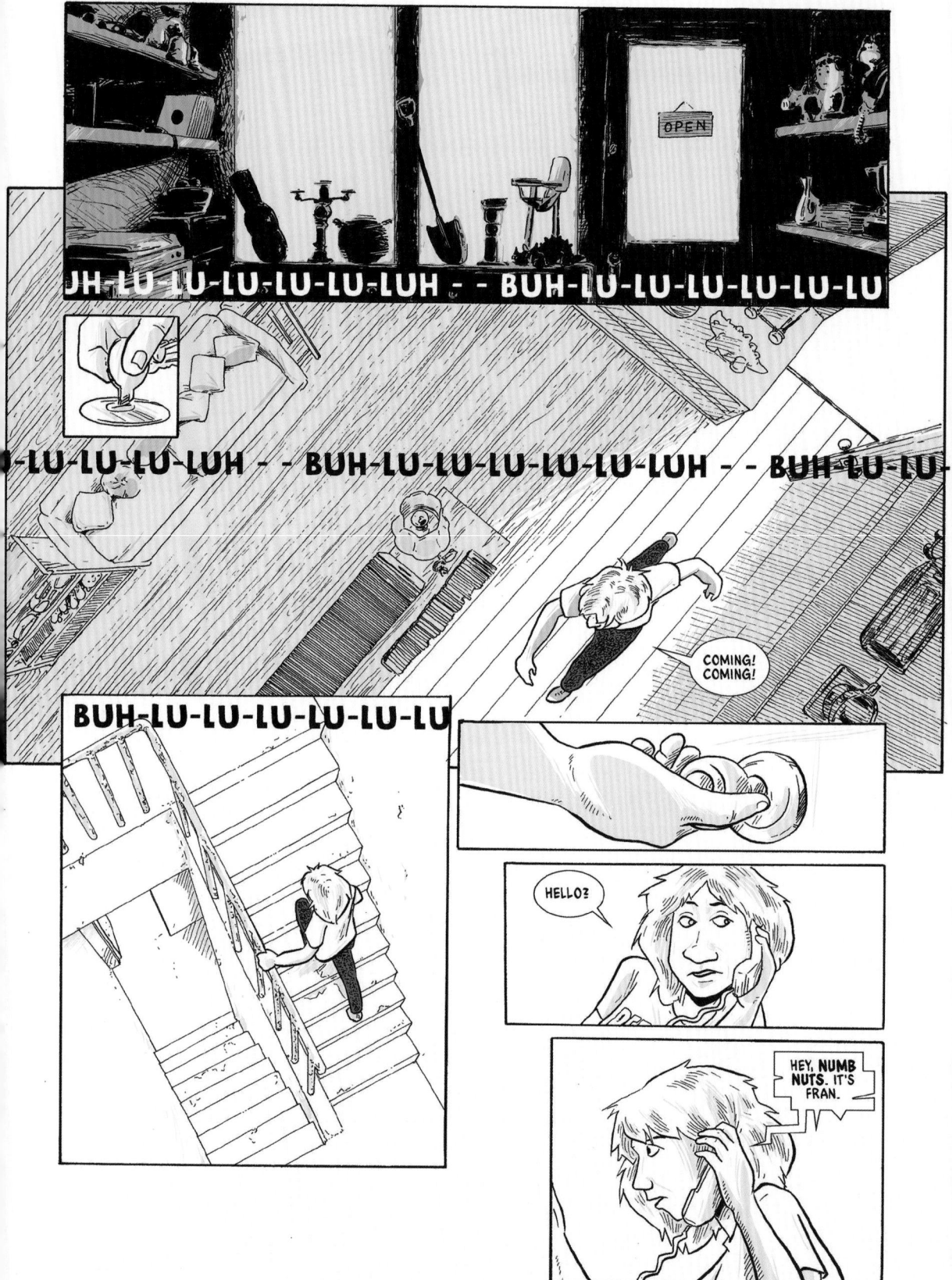

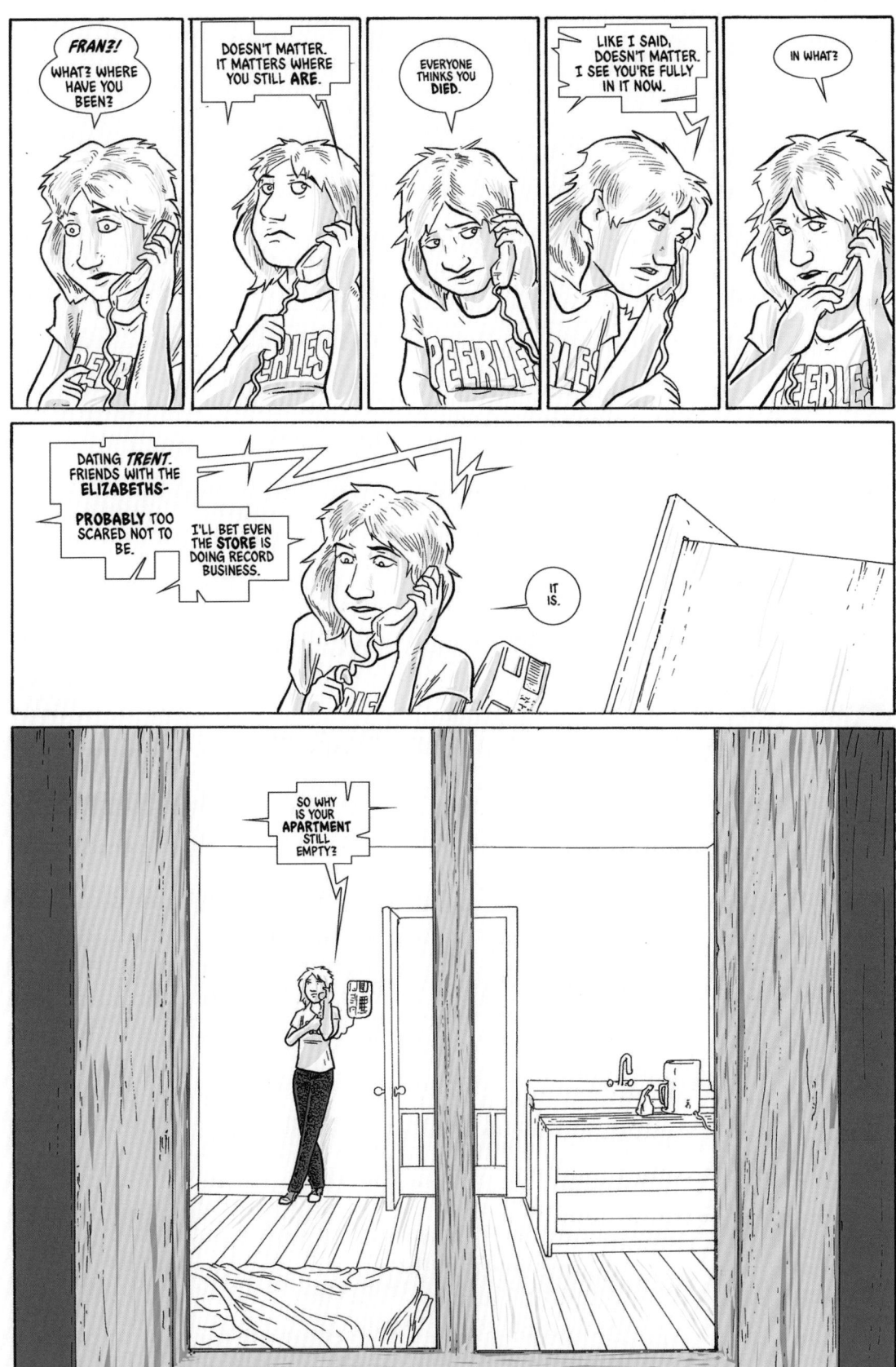

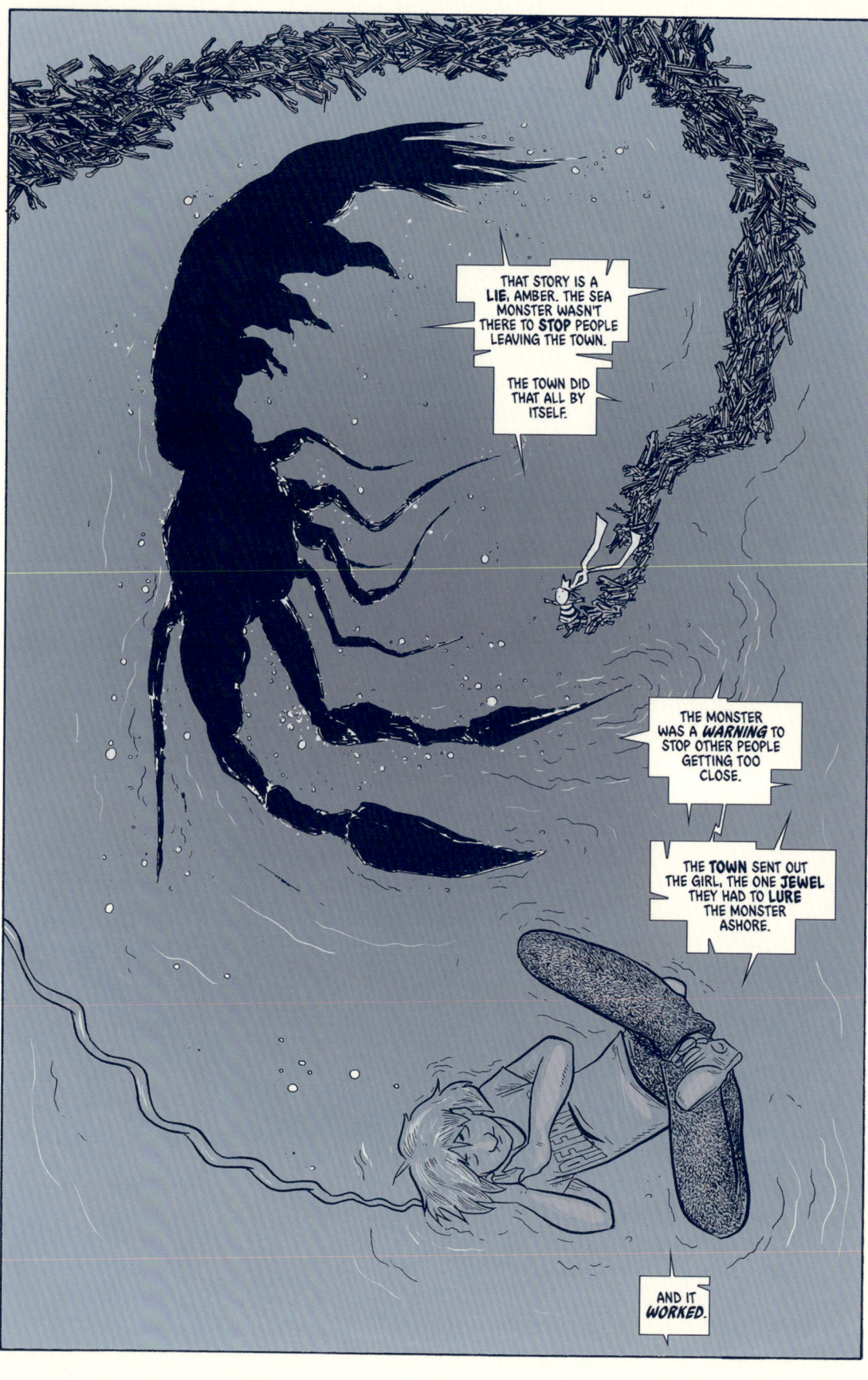

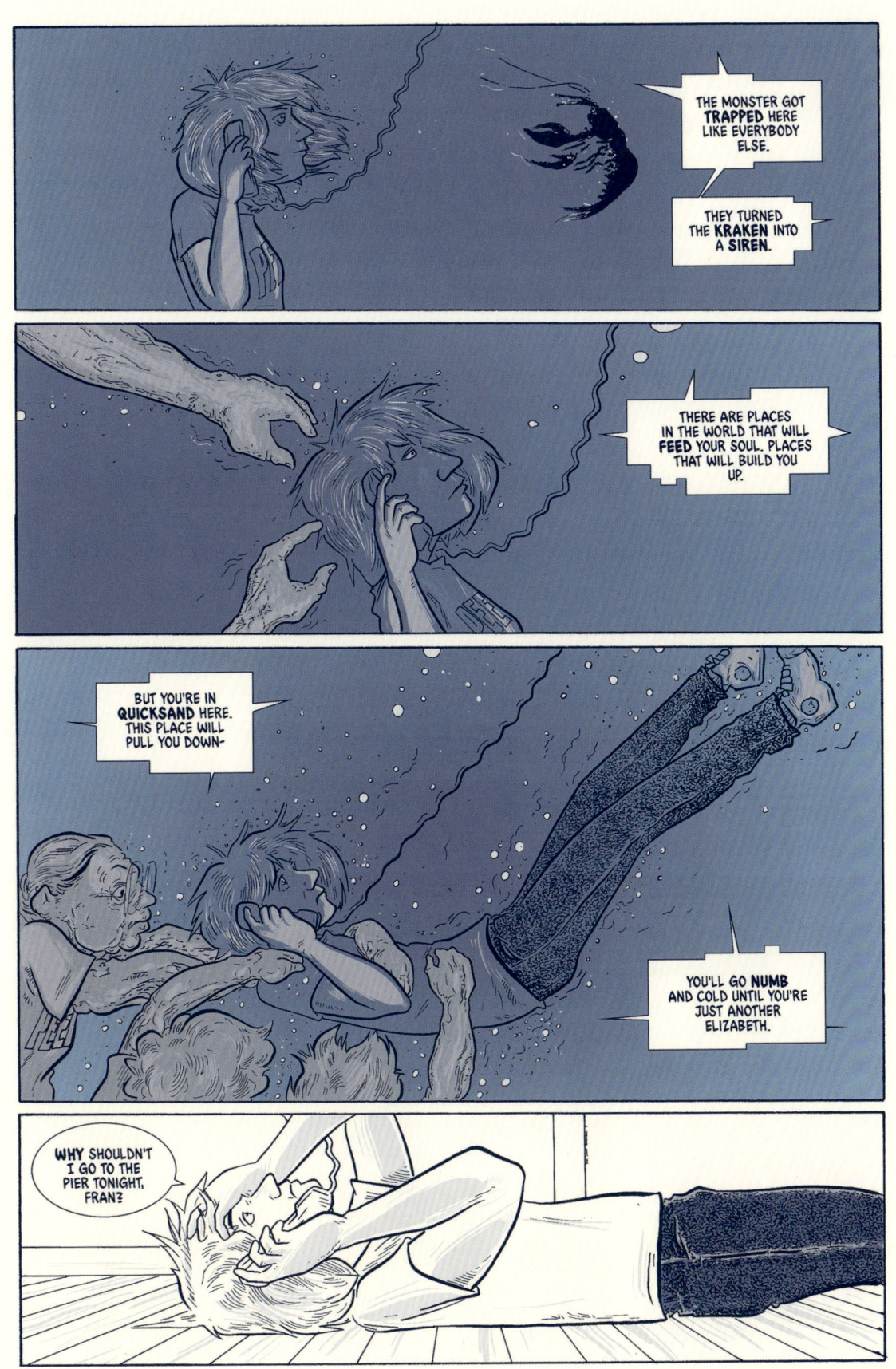

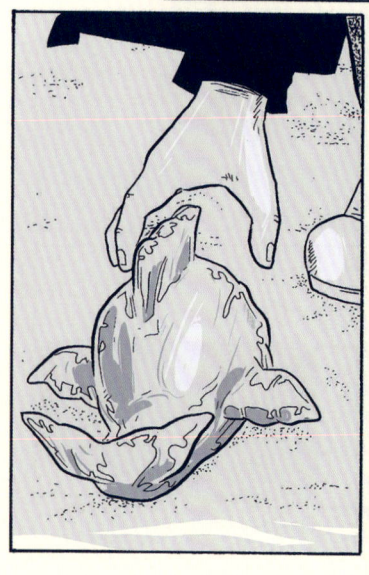

THE END.